Moe THE DOG in Tropical Paradise

by Diane Stanley

Pictures by Elise Primavera

G. P. Putnam's Son's
New York

Library of Congress Cataloging-in-Publication Data

Stanley, Diane. Moe the dog in tropical paradise/by Diane Stanley; illustrated by Elise Primavera.   p.   cm.
Summary: Moe the dog and his friend Arlene can't afford to spend their winter vacation in
Tahiti, so they create their own tropical paradise.
[1. Dogs—Fiction. 2. Vacations—Fiction.] I. Primavera, Elise, ill. II. Title.
PZ7.S7869Mo 1992 [E]—dc20 91-35796 CIP AC

ISBN (hardcover) 0-399-22127-1
10 9 8 7 6 5 4 3
ISBN (Sandcastle) 0-399-22844-6
10 9 8 7 6 5 4 3 2 1
First Impression

For *Joe Armstrong*,
with wishes for sea breezes,
almond trees,
and sand between the toes

—D.S.

Moe the dog was cold. His breath turned to ice on his
whiskers. His ears were warm, but his earmuffs gave him
a headache.

"I can't stand this," he said to his best friend, Arlene.
"A whole week's vacation to sit around and freeze."

"I can't stand it either," Arlene mumbled through her muffler.
"Let's take in a movie."

So they trudged through the snow to see what was playing at
the Roxy.

It turned out to be a double feature: *Polar Voyage* and
Whales of the Arctic. Halfway through the first feature
the heat broke down.

"Can you believe this?" groaned Moe. His popcorn had
frozen solid. "The movies were not a good idea." They left.

Outside, a vendor was selling pretzels and hot cocoa. The cocoa sounded like just the thing, so they both had some. A marshmallow stuck to Arlene's nose, and froze there. Moe laughed. Arlene cried. Moe said he was sorry and gave her a hug. They got the marshmallow off Arlene's nose.

"This day is going from bad to worse," said Moe.

They stopped in front of a travel office. In the window was
a poster. It showed a white sand beach with palm trees.
"Now, that's what we need!" said Moe. "Which would be best:
Tahiti, Hawaii, or the Bahamas?"
Arlene grinned. "Tahiti, definitely!"

They went inside and talked to the travel agent. He told them how much it would cost. Moe sighed. "Maybe some other time," he said.

"I'm feeling pretty discouraged," Arlene said in a discouraged-sounding voice. "I'm going home."

They said good-bye. On the way home, a truck splashed Moe with slush. Then he slipped on an icy patch on the sidewalk. The snow came down more heavily, in big, wet flakes.

Moe was not a happy dog.

When he got home, Moe filled his bathtub with warm water and slid down in it up to his chin. He left out the bubble bath because it reminded him of snow. The feeling began to return to his toes. He thought about palm trees, beaches, and sunshine. Then he had a wonderful idea.

He got dressed and pulled some things out of the attic.

Then he went to Hugo's Building Supply.
And Rembrandt's Art Shop.
And the grocery store.

He worked until late into the night.

The next morning, he called Arlene.

"Hi, Arlene," he said. "It's me, Moe, calling from Tropical
Paradise."

"Wow!" said Arlene, who had a generous heart. "Lucky you!
What's it like?"

"It's warm," said Moe. "There's a gentle breeze. I just went
swimming. Now I'm having a drink by the pool. I have sand
between my toes."

"Oh, Moe," said Arlene, sneezing, "that's wonderful!"

"Yes, it is," said Moe. "Say, Arlene, do me a favor, will you?
I left in a hurry, and I think I left the lights on in my house.
Would you go by and check for me?"

"Sure, Moe," said Arlene.

"Oh, and Arlene—" Moe added, "bring your swimsuit."

Weird! thought Arlene.

Arlene slipped her suit into her purse and put on her coat and boots. She walked through the snow to Moe's house. The lights *were* on. She unlocked the door.

"Surprise!" said Moe. "Welcome to Tropical Paradise!"
"Care for a swim?" he asked.

The next day, Arlene brought flowers, calypso music, and shells. They set up a volleyball net and had a tournament. Arlene made a sarong out of a bedsheet, and she looked very fetching in it. They read books, danced the limbo, and built a sand castle. Moe and Arlene spent all week in Tropical Paradise and neither of them got a sunburn.

"Where shall we go next year?" asked Arlene when the week was up.

"Egypt," said Moe. "I've always wanted to see the pyramids."

"Swell," said Arlene. "We'll save the sand."